MYSTICAL TALES

SHASHWAT SARAOGI

to my parents.....

Contents

Preface — vii

Acknowledgements — ix

1. The Murderer Mystery — 1

2. Judgement Is Served To Everyone — 4

3. The Stag With Long Legs — 8

4. The Deer Hunters — 10

5. The Battle Of The Alarm Clock — 14

6. The Whispers Of The Jungle — 17

7. The Mystery Of Emberstone — 20

8. The Protector — 23

9. The Whispers Of The Trees — 26

10. The Thief From Shadows — 29

11. The Bag Mixup — 32

12. My Dog Ate My Homework (really) — 34

13. The Cat Who Hated Water — 36

Preface

This story was inspired by ideas that formed in my mind sometimes during coversations sometimes during having a shower or while I was on a walk. This book is the culmination or those random thoughts. They helped me express my ideas out in the open world.

Acknowledgements

to my parents, teachers and school who were always by my
side and introduced this platform which helped me through
every step of the book and my friends who gave me
some of the ideas.

ONE

THE MURDERER MYSTERY

The scorching Delhi sun made the air thick and heavy that day. I was already on duty when my phone rang. "The mayor has been found dead. It looks like murder," said the trembling voice. I grabbed my coat and rushed to the mansion.

Chaos greeted me—police, forensic teams, reporters shouting questions. Inside, silence. The air smelled of blood. The mayor lay twisted on the floor, his Kashmiri carpet soaked in red. No broken furniture, no forced entry. A careful killer.

The report was simple. His wife, Ananya, found the body when he didn't show up for breakfast. Deep stab wounds. No fingerprints. The killer wore gloves.

Three people were in the house that night: Ananya, his wife—She claimed she went to bed early after playing tennis. Ramesh, the butler—Said he was cleaning the dusty attic. Arun, the guard—Swore no one entered or left the house, though it was dark.

I checked security footage. Arun's story matched. Then, I

climbed to the attic. It wasn't dusty—it had fresh paint, bright lights. Ramesh hesitated when questioned but I had no proof.

That left Ananya.

At first, she seemed the grieving widow. Tears, shaking hands, soft voice. But cracks appeared. She claimed she left her tennis gear at the club, yet seemed unsure. Then, I found phone messages. She had complained about her husband controlling her, especially after discovering her gambling problem. He had threatened to expose her debts, ruining her reputation.

Confronting her, I saw panic creeping in. Officers got ready. She bolted.

Her heels clacked against marble as she ran. She shoved past officers, almost slipping. Just as she reached the porch, Arun tackled her.

Later, in custody, she refused to speak. But the messages, financial records, and her plans to leave town spoke for her.

At trial, she sat still. The judge spoke of greed, betrayal, her crime. Life in prison.

Walking out of the courthouse, the heat still pressed down, but the real weight was knowing—

The killer wasn't a masked stranger.

It was the person he had trusted the most.

TWO

JUDGEMENT IS SERVED TO EVERYONE

Outside the realm of possibility, a fairy existed who executed the most important and challenging task, which was to either consign a person's soul to heaven or hell. Every single soul that came to him had a mixture of good and bad deeds. This fairy had never failed in his judgment ever since he started doing this duty.

One day, while the fairy was deep in thought sorting souls, a man came trembling. His hands were shaking out of fear, and he was sweating. Fairy, as he does with any other soul, scanned the record without thinking much of the man's fear. And just like that, the absent look on the file shifted to one brimming with shock—the record of the man's life as not introspective thoughts but a horrifying list of sins excluding any possibility for redemption was worse than expected.

"Oh my God!" He plundered. "Of course not in your world!" He let out horrified. He displayed no concern or compassion and just carried on saying; "And did I hear you right? Never once in your entire existence spent breathing did you ever make any good decision?"

The human in front did not have the courage to reply and stand proudly in front the being that was claiming unreversible his judgment. It was clear for him now that there was no escape.

The fairy reached for the lever which would send him plummeting to the destitute pits of hell without any hesitance. But at that very instant, destiny took a turn. As the fairy was slipping, he fell towards what looked like an everlasting white abyss underneath them. He appeared to be stuck in slow motion when he was on the edge of falling.

his wings useless against the suffocating pull of gravity.

"I will lose," he thought as he took refuge deep within a crevice.

"In moments of sheer despair, the last flicker of hope ignites courage like nothing else " He thought to himself as the same man appeared, grasping his arm, withdrawing him from the abyss while straining under the weight of the world conquering gravity.

As he fought with Reality, in utter disbelief the fairy's gaze was fixated onto the man. "Certainly wasn't something from a wish." He commented sheepishly.

"It was just a driving impulse," Distancing himself from the fairy, "With the utmost clarity, it's evident that good is overtaken by evil. Even if I let you go, there remains no difference."

As he rose at a sprint to throw the man down, a firm aura rumbled the skies, splitting the clouds into two while lightning lashed intensively.

zeues decended with lightening stricking the ground to mark his enterance. "This soul, through her actions, proves that even the most unsparing of us, 'A soul that has lived devoid of affection,' can evolve for the better. While we might be forced to endure her she accepted her fate," proclaimed Zeus. "However, fairy, who claim to tip the balance of good and evil, the very essence of weighing does not exist and consider such concepts entirely beyond your comprehension," "That failure is infinitely worse than any possible crime."

His opted to remain silent.

"...Crimes that is no longer your domain," Zeus pronounced, "I will take away that power, fairy, spend your time in hell thinking and pondering about your actions"

Heaven
Hell

THREE

THE STAG WITH LONG LEGS

Once upon a time, there lived a magnificent stag with his charming horns, that he adored above all things. But his long legs are what he despised, He loved to be the center of attention always. One day the stag was roaming around a lush green forest when, he met a squirrel. The squirrel said," Two mean, large men with enormous guns, traps, knifes are out in these parts of the forest and they are trying to find some stags for their horns so run-away dear friend!" Then, he met the monkey he told the same thing as squirrel. Then came a hummingbird, she told the same thing as the monkey. Now the stag was starting to get scared. As soon as the humming bird flew away, the two mean with their enormous guns, traps knife appeared. The stag realized that these are the hunters that all the animals were talking about. He started running very fast with his long legs that he despised. But hunters were on his trial when his beautiful horns that he adored got stuck in the thick spiky thickets. When he got entangled, he knew that he will be caught and that is just what happened. He was caught they took him away they cut his gorgeous horns and that act took his life.

FOUR

THE DEER HUNTERS

When I was a boy, my imagination ran wild. I dreamt of leaping off cliffs on the back of a leopard, of hiding deep in the Amazon rainforest, evading hunters determined to destroy those majestic creatures. My fascination with the wild wasn't just a phase—it grew stronger with every passing year. One day, that dream started to take shape when I joined the Forest Conservation Committee, or FCC.

The training was intense. We trekked through dense forests day and night, built shelters from whatever nature provided, and learned to catch fish using only sticks. Each trek ended with setting up camp alongside our partners, surviving on whatever we could forage or catch. It was exhausting, physically and mentally, but it taught us resilience, teamwork, and how to adapt when the wild refused to be tamed.

After two grueling weeks, we returned to headquarters for the final step: a written exam on wildlife. Only the top twenty scorers would be posted in protected forests to work alongside senior guards and defend the animals we were trained to protect. We studied day and night. When the results were finally posted, I was nervous, hopeful—and stunned. I had ranked second. All the pain, sweat, and sleepless nights had paid off.

I returned home to celebrate with family and friends. My parents begged me to stay longer, but I couldn't. My new assignment was calling, and I was eager to meet the people I'd be working with—and the forest I had only imagined as a child.

Two flights took me to Manaus, a city in north-western Brazil, where our temporary headquarters was set up. The forest wasn't far. A small stream flowed beside our base, and we used it for everything—drinking, fishing, bathing. Mango, chestnut, cherry, and bamboo trees surrounded us, and when we tired of eating fish, we chewed bamboo just to break the monotony.

Every morning, we woke at dawn and bathed under a makeshift shower—a bamboo pipe and a plastic bag, ingeniously rigged together. After breakfast, we piled into jeeps and headed into the forest. The road, if you could call it that, was barely navigable. After a while, we left the vehicles behind to avoid attracting predators—jaguars, leopards, green anacondas, and poison dart frogs.

We hiked three miles in. My legs ached, and a stinging pain stopped me in my tracks. One side of my leg had swollen up like a balloon. At first, the seniors thought it was a killer bee sting, but back at camp, they discovered something far more alarming—a poison dart. The kind used by hunters to tranquilize big cats. It had been aimed at me.

They treated me quickly, and thankfully, I recovered fast. But the next morning, our seniors delivered chilling news: the dart hadn't been a random accident. I had been deliberately targeted. We were ordered to be extra cautious—and given a new mission: tag as many big cats as possible to track their movement and protect them from poachers.

We split into two teams, each with senior guides, trainees, food supplies, radios, GPS trackers, and first aid kits. Our bags felt like they weighed a thousand pounds. Two miles from the jungle's edge, we split directions—our team went east, the other west. We avoided the main trails, keeping low and silent.

After hours of searching, we had seen nothing—until we spotted a hunter. He was preparing to shoot a leopard. We moved in quietly, tackled him, and tied him up. I radioed our coordinates to the other team—but before I could say another word, everything went black.

I woke up in a hospital bed.

A second hunter had ambushed me. But thanks to the GPS tracker, our reinforcements had found us in time. They subdued the attacker and got me to safety.

I was lucky. And I was more determined than ever. The wild wasn't just a dream anymore—it was my responsibility. The creatures I once imagined riding through the trees were real, and now, I was their protector.

FIVE

THE BATTLE OF THE ALARM CLOCK

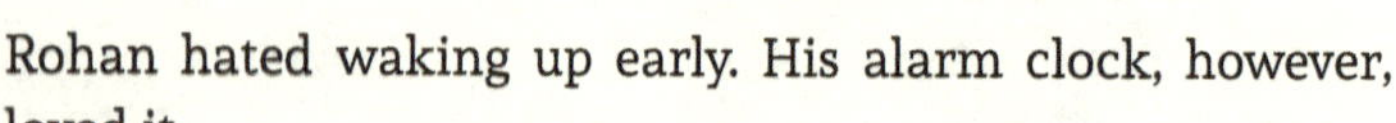

Rohan hated waking up early. His alarm clock, however, loved it.

Every morning at 6:00 AM, the clock buzzed loudly. BEEP! BEEP! BEEP!

Rohan groaned, grabbed a pillow, and threw it at the clock.

The clock fell—but kept buzzing. Annoyed, Rohan picked it up and put it in a drawer.

The next morning: BEEP! BEEP! BEEP! From inside the drawer.

Rohan glared at it. He put it in his closet.

Next morning:

BEEP! BEEP! BEEP!

Muffled, but still annoying.

Rohan had enough. He carried the clock outside.

He placed it in the fridge.

The next morning:

BEEP! BEEP! BEEP!

From inside the fridge.

His mom screamed, "Why is there an alarm in the fridge?!"

Rohan groaned.

Defeated, he took the clock out.

He stared at it.

The clock stared back.

Rohan sighed.

"Fine. You win."

And for the first time ever, Rohan woke up on time.

SIX

THE WHISPERS OF THE JUNGLE

Deep within the emerald folds of the Amazon rainforest, where sunlight trickled through thick canopies and the air pulsed with the rhythm of unseen wings and rustling leaves, lived a young ocelot named Tiko. His golden coat, marked with ink-black marks, helped him melt into the dappled shadows of the jungle floor.

Tiko was smaller than most of the other predators, but he was quick, clever, and curious—dangerously curious, some would say. Unlike the older ocelots who stayed close to familiar trails and knew when to stay still, Tiko was always chasing the wind, the sound of something new.

One misty morning, he was perched on a low branch, eyes narrowed, ears twitching. Something was different. The birds weren't singing, and even the monkeys, usually so noisy at dawn, were silent. Then he heard it—a soft hum, unnatural and strange, coming from deeper in the forest than he had ever dared venture.

Compelled, Tiko slipped silently through vines and leaves, moving like a shadow. The hum grew louder, now mixed with mechanical clatters and sharp human voices. He paused at the edge of a clearing and crouched low.

Machines. Big yellow beasts of metal were chewing through trees with brutal teeth. Men in helmets shouted over the roar, directing the destruction. Tiko's heart pounded. He had heard the stories—the whispers from the toucans and the murmurs from old jaguars—about humans and the machines that turned the living jungle into dust.

Tiko's paws itched to run, but something else caught his eye: a young capuchin monkey, no bigger than a coconut, clinging to a branch right above the chaos. It had likely strayed from its troop, too young to understand the danger. A branch snapped. The monkey shrieked and fell, landing hard just inches from the spinning jaws of a machine.

Without thinking, Tiko sprang.

He darted into the clearing like a streak of light. The humans shouted, startled. Tiko ignored them. He grabbed the tiny monkey gently in his jaws and leapt over a fallen log just as the machine's teeth sliced the air where he had stood.

Back in the safety of the trees, the capuchin clung to his neck, trembling. Tiko didn't stop until they were miles away, deep in a quiet glade where the air smelled only of leaves and water.

The monkey chirped softly, curling up beside Tiko. For the first time, the young ocelot felt something warm and unfamiliar—a quiet pride. He hadn't just survived the jungle that day; he had protected it.

From then on, the animals whispered Tiko's name with respect. He became a silent guardian, always watching, always listening. And while the machines kept coming, so did the stories of the brave ocelot who ran into danger not for glory, but because he understood that the jungle wasn't just his home—it was everyone's.

SEVEN

THE MYSTERY OF EMBERSTONE

Deep within the dense jungles of Emberwood, where ancient trees towered like silent guardians, lay the legendary city of Emberstone. No map marked its location, no explorer had ever returned to tell its tale. It was a place of myth, whispered about in secret circles, where treasures beyond imagination were said to be hidden.

Aria, a fearless explorer, had spent years chasing rumors of Emberstone. Guided by an old, half-burnt manuscript she had discovered in a forgotten library, she embarked on her most dangerous expedition yet. With her trusted partner Kai—a skilled tracker—by her side, they ventured deep into the uncharted jungle, overcoming treacherous terrain, venomous creatures, and eerie echoes that seemed to warn them away.

One evening, as the sun dipped below the horizon and painted the jungle in fiery hues, Aria and Kai stumbled upon a colossal stone gate covered in intricate carvings. It matched the descriptions from the manuscript. Their hearts raced. With careful precision, Aria pressed a sequence of symbols, and the gate groaned open, revealing a breathtaking city illuminated by thousands of glowing emberstones.

Golden towers stretched into the sky, their surfaces shimmering like liquid fire. The air hummed with ancient magic, and in the center of it all lay the Heart of Emberstone—an artifact rumored to grant its wielder unimaginable knowledge and power.

As Aria stepped forward, the city trembled. The ancient guardians—statues of stone and flame—awakened, their hollow eyes burning with warning. It was then that she realized the truth: Emberstone wasn't a treasure to be claimed. It was a secret meant to remain hidden.

With seconds to spare, Aria and Kai sprinted back through the gate as the city began to collapse, returning to the jungle's embrace. The gate sealed behind them, the jungle swallowing all traces of Emberstone once more.

Though they left empty-handed, Aria carried with her the greatest discovery of all—the proof that legends were real. And some mysteries were best left untouched.

EIGHT

THE PROTECTOR

The sun filtered through the dense jungle canopy as 12-year-old Maya tightened her grip on the old map she found in her grandfather's attic. Faded with time and marked with strange symbols, it pointed to a spot deep in the heart of the Amazon—where something called "The Heart of the Jungle" lay hidden.

Armed with a compass, her dog Tito, and her endless curiosity, Maya trekked through vines, leapt over creeks, and listened to the calls of birds she couldn't name. The jungle seemed alive, whispering secrets with every rustle of leaves.

Suddenly, Tito growled. A shape moved in the shadows—it was a jaguar, eyes glowing gold. Maya stood frozen, heart pounding. But instead of attacking, the jaguar simply stared, then turned and slowly walked away, looking back as if to say, "Follow me."

She did.

After hours of following the silent guide, Maya stumbled into a clearing. In the center stood a massive tree, its roots twisting like serpents and its trunk carved with ancient symbols—the same ones from the map.

She pressed her hand to the bark. The tree glowed faintly, then cracked open at the base to reveal a hidden chamber. Inside, glowing crystals pulsed like a heartbeat, and a small stone figurine sat on a pedestal. The Heart of the Jungle.

As she picked it up, the jungle hushed. Then, the wind whispered through the leaves—"Protector."

Maya smiled. The jungle had chosen her.

NINE

THE WHISPERS OF
THE TREES

The jungle was alive.

Every leaf shimmered with dew, every branch trembled with secrets. Alex had never meant to get lost—one wrong turn during the expedition, and now the dense canopy swallowed all signs of the path. But fear quickly gave way to awe.

A burst of color flashed—scarlet macaws leapt into the sky. Somewhere deeper in the undergrowth, a howler monkey called out, echoing through the trees. Alex pushed forward, machete in hand, sweat running down his neck. The air was thick, humming with life.

Suddenly, he stumbled into a clearing. In its center stood an ancient stone structure, half-swallowed by vines and moss. He froze. This wasn't on any map. Glyphs danced across the stone, telling a story long forgotten.

A soft rustling behind him. Alex turned quickly—eyes meeting the gaze of a jaguar, golden and still. Heart pounding, he remembered what the guide had said: Don't run. They stared at each other, man and beast, both part of the wild now.

Then, as suddenly as it appeared, the jaguar turned and vanished into the brush. The moment lingered like a dream. Alex let out a breath, a shaky grin spreading across his face.

He wasn't just lost. He was somewhere sacred, somewhere real.

When he finally found his way back to camp, his teammates rushed over. "Where've you been?"

Alex just smiled. "Out there," he said, pointing to the trees

TEN

THE THIEF FROM SHADOWS

Under the dim light of a flickering streetlamp, Rohan moved like a shadow through the busy city. His hands were quick, his eyes sharp. People whispered his name—Silver Shadow. But he didn't steal for money. He stole for the thrill, for the challenge... and maybe for something deeper he couldn't quite name.

One night, he set his sights on the Taj Mahal, a grand palace where an old silver locket was locked away. People said it held a map to hidden treasure. Rohan, always chasing a dream, couldn't resist.

The city was alive with music, laughter, and barking dogs. But Rohan moved quietly through the dark, slipping past guards and traps with ease. He finally reached the room where the locket was kept. It sat in a glass case, glowing in the moonlight. He picked the lock, opened the case, and reached for it.

Then a voice stopped him.

"You're bold," said Meera, the young heiress of the Mahal. She stood behind him, calm and curious.

Rohan hadn't expected this.

Meera wore a white robe, her eyes sharp but not angry. Instead of calling the guards, she walked closer and asked, "You could've stolen anything. Why this?"

Rohan answered without thinking. "A thief always looks for something lost."

She smiled slightly. "And what have you lost ?"

He didn't know. He had taken many things, but none of them had ever meant anything.

Meera looked at the locket. "It's not a map," she said. "It belonged to my mother."

Rohan looked at her. She sounded sad, not angry.

"Then why do you keep it locked away?" he asked.

"Because it reminds me of what I lost," she said softly. "And sometimes, the past is too heavy to carry."

They stood in silence. In that moment, Rohan understood—he wasn't the only one searching for something.

He closed the case and stepped back. "Some things are meant to be found, not stolen," he said.

Meera nodded slowly.

That night, the Silver Shadow vanished into the city. But he left behind more than he took. And in the quiet halls of the palace, Meera held the locket closer, wondering if some lost things could still be found.

ELEVEN
THE BAG MIXUP

It was a normal Monday morning. Riya grabbed her school bag, ran out the door, and jumped into the school bus, just in time.

At school, she sat in her class, ready for math. The teacher said, "Take out your homework."

Riya opened her bag... and froze.

Inside were two bananas, a toy dinosaur, a pair of socks, and a note that said:
"Don't forget to feed the goldfish. – Mom"

"This... is not my bag," Riya whispered.

Her best friend, Meena, leaned over. "Why do you have a T. rex in there?"

"I think I took my little brother's bag!"

Just then, the school office called. "Riya, please come to the front. Your mom is here."

When she got there, her mom was holding Riya's real school bag—and laughing.

Apparently, Riya's three-year-old brother, Aarav, had packed his bag to "go to work" like Riya. He had even placed a banana as "lunch" and the toy dinosaur for "protection."

"Looks like Aarav's ready for a business meeting at Jurassic Park," the principal joked.

Riya and her mom switched bags, and Riya ran back to class.

Later that day, Aarav was found in the living room wearing sunglasses, holding a spoon like a microphone, saying, "I'm the boss now!"

From that day on, Riya always double-checked her bag before leaving.

And Aarav? He still packs a bag every morning. Just in case he gets called for a dinosaur emergency.

TWELVE

MY DOG ATE MY HOMEWORK (REALLY)

Last week, something unbelievable happened.

Rohan was sitting at the table, finishing his science homework. His dog, Bruno, was lying under the table, being unusually quiet. That should have been the first warning.

Rohan finished his last sentence, yawned, and went to get a snack. When he came back... the homework was gone.

Only tiny, chewed-up paper pieces remained on the floor—and Bruno was sitting in the corner, wagging his tail proudly, with a bit of paper stuck to his nose.

"Bruno!" Rohan shouted. "You ate my homework!"

Bruno just blinked, then burped.

Rohan picked up the leftover paper and sighed. "No one's going to believe this."

The next morning at school, Rohan stood in front of the teacher.

"Ma'am," he said, "my dog ate my homework."

The class burst out laughing. Even the teacher smiled. "That's the oldest excuse in the book, Rohan."

"But it's true!" he said. "Look, I brought the evidence!"

He held out a plastic bag full of chewed-up paper bits. Some even had drool on them. The teacher looked shocked... and a little grossed out.

"Well," she said, holding the bag away from her face, "this is... creative. You'll still have to do it again, but I'll give you an extra day."

The next day, Rohan turned in a fresh copy—with a small note at the bottom:
"P.S. Bruno is banned from homework time."

Now, Bruno is only allowed near toys, not papers.

But every time Rohan does homework, Bruno still watches.... licking his lips like he is waiting for dessert.

THIRTEEN

THE CAT WHO HATED WATER

Mira loved her cat, Simba. He was soft, fluffy, and very, very lazy. He slept 20 hours a day and only moved when he smelled tuna.

There was just one problem: Simba hated water.

Not disliked. Hated.

So when Mira's mom said, "Simba needs a bath today," Mira knew it would be a big problem.

She gently picked him up, carried him to the bathroom, and turned on the tap.

Simba opened one eye. Suspicious.

Mira slowly placed him near the tub.

Simba opened both eyes. Alert.

She touched his paw to the water.

Poof! He turned into a ninja.

He jumped out of her hands, ran out of the bathroom, slid across the hallway rug, and hid under the sofa like a fluffy pancake.

It took Mira, her mom, and a piece of chicken to pull him out. They tried again.

This time, Mira wore a raincoat and goggles. Her mom wore oven mitts. Simba wore a look of pure anger.

In the end, they managed to give him a half-bath. The front half was clean, the back half got away.

Simba refused to look at them for two days. He sat with his back turned, tail twitching like he was writing angry messages in the air.

But on the third day, he forgave them. Mira gave him a full bowl of tuna and let him sleep on her pillow.

Now, every time someone says the word "bath," Simba disappears under the table.

And Mira? She learned one important lesson Never try to bathe a cat without snacks, speed, and safety gear.

To every reader who made it to this final page — thank you.

Writing a book is a deeply personal journey, but it's only when someone reads it that the story truly comes to life. Whether this book made you think, feel, laugh, cry, or simply kept you company for a little while, I'm grateful you gave it your time. There are countless stories out there, and the fact that you chose this one means more than I can say. I hope it stayed with you in some way — even if just a line, a moment, or a feeling.

Thank you for being part of this journey.

With all my heart,